Unexpected Short Tales of Surprise

P. A. Farrell

Unexpected Short Tales of Surprise

P. A. Farrell

Published by Dr. Patricia A. Farrell, 2023.

UNEXPECTED SHORT TALES OF SURPRISE

First edition. October 6, 2023.

Copyright © 2023 P. A. Farrell.

ISBN: 979-8223423010

Written by P. A. Farrell.

Table of Contents

Copyright

A MOTHER'S PRAYER

A piercing morning sun promised no relief but only more heat as the carefully tanned woman stood waiting with the little girl in her overly heavy dress and orthopedic shoes. The woman was sporting faux haute couture in crisp white shorts and a mind-blowing bright blue halter, her blonde hair carefully arranged in a silky ponytail. Delicate leather sandals with a troublesome strap were a bit loose, but she loved the look.

Sunglasses, not Bentley Platinum but knockoffs, shielded her eyes from the sun's glare. The little girl, refusing to hold the woman's hand, squinted in the painful light and squirmed, scraping the bottom of her brace on the cement. No attention was paid to her discomfort.

The doorman's heel crunched on tiny pebbles as he twisted to turn away, seeming not to notice the activity at the curb. He had done his duty. Now it was up to the new mother.

A bus would arrive within minutes, but to the woman at the curb, it seemed an eternity. Looking down at the little girl, she flashed her carefully practiced non-Duchenne smile, which had always so usefully connoted her feigned joy in the past. Mirrors had helped a lot. The smile was the key to her most recent success.

A short yellow bus slid up to the curb. The bus stopped, a large stop sign flipped out, and two young women jumped to the sidewalk. The bus was unmarked, but the yellow t-shirts the women wore had an emblem of a day camp.

Now the yellow-shirted women greeted the woman and the child and with great enthusiasm, began bending over and smiling, clapping their hands in unison in an excessive display of joy; frantic rather than heartfelt. The little girl looked at the three of them and kept her hands at her sides.

The blue-halter-garbed woman became more animated as the little girl jumped up and down with effort in a show of dissatisfaction, her face distorted and now dappled with tears.

"No, no, no! I don't want to go!" The pleading would gain her nothing. Her fate was sealed. The fees were paid, she was registered, and she'd get on the bus, eventually. The woman had no doubt of it.

"Florence, honey, it's going to be fun. You'll meet other children who will play with you, and you'll get to make friends. You want friends, don't you?"

Forcing herself not to grit her teeth, the woman was wondering if she might order the camp workers to lift the little girl up onto the bus. No, her husband wouldn't like that. It's too soon to upset him.

Concerned that she would be late for her Pilates class, the woman initiated a vigorous few minutes of coaxing in an effort to thaw the reluctance. Photos, photos were needed to memorialize the special occasion, and the woman began taking them with her phone.

One, two, ten photos taken next to the bus, several with the young women, and the little girl leaning against the bus. Excessive waving of goodbyes began now as the girl mounted the bus stairs with some assistance.

The stop sign retracts. The woman's frantic waving continues as the bus wends its way from the curb. More smiles and waving from the curb. The bus enters traffic and slides slowly away, disappearing like a yellow bug in the crush of morning traffic.

The woman crosses the street, fingers her phone and begins talking as she views herself on the video display. Her hair, eyebrows, and make-up all look good to her.

The traffic light turns red. She never looks up, as is her usual carefree way of crossing streets, busy or otherwise.

Traffic was supposed to stop for her, wasn't it? Talking on her phone, she crossed the next corner as the traffic light turned red. The leather sandal strap slips. She slows down to wiggle her foot.

"The doorman had to help me," she fairly moans, "because she didn't want to leave the building, and she was grabbing onto the door and everything she could find. Why, God, oh, God, why me? Oh, God, I'm so sick of her. Thank God she got on the bus!" The pesky sandal strap slips again, but a quick hop will re-secure it.

"You have no idea what I had to do with that kid. It was his week with her. He's at work so I had to take her to the bus today. Can you beat that? Oh, my God, I ..."

Hanging in mid-air, the sentence would never be completed as a screech of tire on asphalt ripped the muggy morning air. Blue collided with blue.

"Johanna? Johanna?" The voice fades as the phone begins an acrobatic swan dive in the air before it crashes into the roadway, shattering as it does.

The faux Bentley glasses follow the phone in short order.

Yes, the traffic had stopped for her.

COURTESY NEVER DIES

No one told me I would use a walker, hunched over those curved aluminum handles and hoping the brakes on the wheels would hold, but that's life. You never know what it's going to throw at you, and you've got to be ready to catch it with both hands and draw it toward your chest so it doesn't fall to the floor. But today, the bus jostled, slamming me into a pole. A man sneered at me. "They shouldn't let people like you on the bus!" Yeah, people like me with walkers.

A slow slog from the bus stop sends stabs of pain to my ankle, but I push on. Good thing my folding friend has wheels. I don't think I could pick it up. Each slab of the sidewalk is daring me forward. The beast is waiting, and I've got to gather my strength, so I take it slowly to save my breath and prepare.

I see it up ahead of me. The carpet of cement stretches out like a raceway that will never see a race. Seven stone demons wait to test me again, as they do each time I approach. A slender handrail is my only hope, and then the door, which becomes heavier each day, awaits to laugh in my face, daring me to open it. So much malevolence, so much evil.

Stopping at the first step, I pin an imaginary medal on myself for making it this far. The staircase is empty. Not a person around who might wring out some small bit of kindness to help me. The walker waits like a babe to be pulled up behind me. I hate it and what it signifies about me and what I've lost. But the aluminum babe and I make it this time.

I look up in tired expectation, and an apparition stands before me. Dressed in clothing that long ago lost its style, a jacket that is more robe than a suit jacket, he is a caricature out of a Dickens tale.

Wiry thin white hairs give him the look of a fuzzy halo. His large nose almost disappears into the pudgy face, now marked with a smile. The slight twinkle in his cloudy eyes is reassuring.

Wrinkled, rumpled, and over 90, he stands holding on to his cane as he utters, "Here, let me hold the door for you," and pushes his entire back, not his hand, against it to supply the strength he needs. I see how he digs his heels in to provide a hold on the door that demands to be shut in my face. Evil door. I hate it and the stairs and the walker. I hate all of them.

But courtesy and human kindness haven't died, at least not in one frail, elderly man, and I will accept.

THE IMAGINARY LIBRARIAN

Brushing a stray hair above her ear into the severe bun she wears, she sits on her polished wooden chair behind her plain wooden desk and busies herself straightening folders, shifting papers, and gazing at the boxes lining the walls up to the top of the imaginary ceiling.

Some bindings on the imaginary books may need a bit of tending, but that's not something she needs to worry about. She waits for the commands she knows will come, and when they do, she will be ready to rise and shuffle across the floor in her sensible shoes.

An alarm rings and she shoots up the ladder to the top shelf where the most worn books are held and retrieves a bit of information needed by the reader. A creaking sound greets her every step up and down the ladder. Snatching the bit in the book, she scoots down and pushes it into the pneumatic tube. Task completed, she retreats to her desk and adjusts her green eyeshade. Her job is almost finished, but she refuses to think about it.

"Yes, yes, for a moment he almost seemed to come back as you asked him about that childhood memory. Funny how those things can be retrieved," the man in the white physician's coat mumbles to an intern as they hover over the bed.

"It won't be long now," the physician continues.

The vigil is almost complete as ninety years of life slip away in the quiet of the early morning light. The librarian's job will be completed before the sun comes up fully. Slowly, the sheet is drawn over the closed eyes.

OUR KIND

The hiss and steady, low thumping of machines assaulted the hallway air. White uniformed men and women, occasionally one in a black smock and pants, cruised throughout. What type of shoes do they wear? They make no noise except for an occasional squeak when they stop abruptly.

One figure stood out. The black outfit with the stiff white collar told it all.

"We rarely get many of our kind in here," he said almost gleefully. Not one to push back from a table, the man in black waddled to the bedside.

"I read your name on the roster and saw that you were one of us, so I came to comfort you in your time of need."

Did I want to pray with him now or should he offer prayers for me tomorrow morning?

Feeling a bit off-kilter thanks to the meds they had given me to relax and sleep, I murmured, "Tomorrow will be fine. Thank you very much." The etiquette lessons taught instead of science so long ago kicked in without a thought. Did I want prayers? Did I need prayers? I doubted it, but they were being freely offered, so what the hell, fire away, dear man, fire away.

"Oh, don't thank me. I want to do this for you." In truth, he eagerly sought anyone to pray for in this particular hospital, and here was one candidate. The delight he felt at being released from his stuffy office downstairs was difficult to contain. He so wanted to sit and comfort this patient and coax her to pray with him.

"I have rosary beads. Would you prefer we say the rosary?"

Even dinner would have to wait tonight. The thought of luscious chicken, shining gravy dripping all over it, the special vegetables that the cook had prepared for him, and the exquisitely delightful and frothy rich dessert that was now sitting in the refrigerator was almost too much to resist, but he must resist.

How often would one of his kind be here on the surgical floor and require his care? It was his sworn duty, the duty he accepted over 40 years ago when he lay before the altar and the sacrament was upon him. No, he could not allow himself the delights of the dinner table.

Yes, it would be a sacrifice, but he must make it and, perhaps, it would be to his benefit in the afterlife if he undertook this latest charge.

Lying there in the bed, looking at this plump man almost bouncing with happiness who was offering to pray for my safe delivery from surgery was something I didn't want to think about, but he was here.

What could I do with him now to get him to leave? If he left, I could quickly dispatch my small dinner tray, turn on the TV and then drift quietly off to sleep until the morning.

He couldn't possibly understand my conflict with etiquette and annoyance. How could he? He lived most of his life in an extremely cloistered existence, but he enjoyed several pleasures bestowed upon him by wealthy patients who appreciated his good services.

I knew these men from childhood. They had the most expensive stereo equipment in the area, a fairly nice car that was given to them and they were whisked away to ultra-chic vacation homes in the Hamptons with only the slightest hint that they would enjoy a bit of time away from the hospital.

Not only did this man have patients who wished to curry favor because they felt he had special intervention with God, but he also had a small terrier dog. But no dogs were allowed in the hospital.

"Well, I'll be leaving now," he uttered, almost like a child who wouldn't get his wish. "I'll be praying for you" Turning, he left and waved a final goodbye at the doorway with the small metal container affixed to the side of it.

A nurse came walking in.

"Ok," the nurse announced, "tomorrow you're all set for your blepharoplasty, the eyelid lift you wanted."

Well, who knows, maybe eyelid lifts need prayers, too.

TUNA SANDWICH EMPATHY

A ball of blinding light is rising across the river, sending its rays streaming through the windows and over the highly polished floors and into every cranny of this lonely waiting area.

Silence, no music, no voices, nothing will comfort one who sits and waits. The space is devoid of any thoughtful comforts. The waiting goes on, undisturbed.

A young woman, her hair casually combed, dressed simply in jeans and a soft silk blouse, is sitting in this hollow room with its scattered, years-old magazines sporting torn covers, empty, crushed coffee cups tossed into half-filled garbage cans and stained, overstuffed chairs that keep secrets well. A hint of acrid antiseptic fills the still air in the room.

No distracting TVs showing news programs or game shows, no playing cards or even music to relieve the tension. Not a thought had been given to ease the mental pain of the insufferable waiting. Large wall clocks seem reluctant to move.

Sitting hunched forward, the woman permits herself to only unclench her hands when picking at her fingernails. Her bloodshot eyes are almost bolted to the door with the warning sign prohibiting entrance.

Fashionable sneakers drive a frown of discomfort and she realizes she's forgotten to wear socks. A fresh weeping blister is emerging on her heel. But she puts that aside. It's a small price to pay for a dear friend in a dangerous situation. Guilt or discomfort would be self-indulgent and this is no time for it. There have been times to be selfish, to be the life of the party, but today that seems so long ago. A laugh would be a sob now and she must be strong and resist, as best she can, to keep only one person, one thought in mind, and that dreaded word, surgery, echoes like a pebble in a tin can in her head.

Now the morgue-like silence is broken by an elderly couple. They shuffle in and begin looking at their phones as soon as they fall into seats. The man brushes his long white beard aside as he removes his hat and gazes at the screen. No expression, no words. The older woman, after first securing the strands of hair that escaped from her tight, woven beret, already has a conversation going. Her clothing is telling: the long, full skirt, and the drab, cotton stockings that cover her legs, just as her husband's beard is an indication of beliefs. There is an occasional, muffled, not cheerful, laugh as she responds, "Yes, again today."

She looks up after a half hour, smiles, turns to her husband, and after saying something in a foreign language, they get up.

They disappear down a broad, carpeted staircase. Then they return, carrying two small brown paper bags.

Extending her hand with one bag in it, the older woman says to the young woman, "You look like you could use something to eat. It's a tuna sandwich with a pickle. Take it."

A murmur of thanks. The sandwich is partially eaten in silence. Then, a short conversation begins about why they are all there.

With drooping eyes and a slight turn of the head, the older woman indicates the door with the sign. "I didn't want him to go skiing, but he wanted to go so badly, we let him. He hit a tree. Permanent brain damage. We bring him for scheduled brain surgery twice a year. I think it's pressure, but we don't understand."

The couple moves unhurriedly and invites the young woman to meet their son in the surgery waiting area. The forbidden door is opened by the old man, as though he has special authority.

Lying in the bed, his eyes rolling around uncontrollably, like small blue balls implanted in his head, the young man cannot speak and is drooling.

"This is Daniel, our son." It's more of a lament than a statement.

His face is expressionless and the rolling eyes never stop for a second in their incessant movement around the room.

Behind the silent, searching, and somber face framed by thick black curly hair is a prisoner held captive by a brain that refuses to function normally, and that in turn holds his parents prisoners, as well. It will be so until they die. Then who will watch, care, and bring him for surgery until the day he is finally released?

The introductions are over. A young surgeon signals it's time for the young man to be taken to the operating room. The group of three slowly and quietly disintegrates. The parents are led soundlessly away. But the memory of a tuna sandwich will remain as a rye-bread tribute to empathy.

Before they move off, the mother stops for a moment, reaches out for an almost imperceptible touch of her hand on the young woman's arm, and then she turns to follow the surgeon. The couple disappears in the gray gloom of the hallway like ghosts in the young woman's imagination.

As she walks alone down the hospital hallway, the young woman hears the sounds of laughter coming from a nearby room. She peeks in and sees a family gathered, sharing stories and supporting each other through their difficult time. There is a sense of community and belonging, but she realizes that sometimes we make the most meaningful connections without words at all.

TRAVELS BY MYSELF

The harried young woman looms over her ten-year-old son, saying, firmly, "You have until the end of this flight to do your homework. And don't talk to me like that. I won't stand for it."

Since I was scrambling to stuff my luggage anywhere I could, I hadn't heard the "talking to her" that had gone on. I had to secure one of those all-too-scarce overhead bins for my carry-on luggage. Most bins appeared to be full. People entering took the first bin they saw, never caring if it wasn't for their seat.

"I don't know why you get so upset." He's pouting now. Head down, he looks like a child who may not grow up to be a very pleasant adult. She's continuing her diatribe and this poor boy must sit and listen. I'll bet she's a stepmother and he's wondering why someone doesn't save him from her. Still, he makes no response to her railing.

"Don't talk to me like that. Just get to doing your homework."

The din dies down as the flight attendant goes through the cabin, closing the overhead compartments with a resolute slam that tells all they're full.

"Is that a bag there?" Sweat appears on the flight attendant's face. A twist of the head and pursing of the lips indicate the true intention of the question. "Are these your things? You can hold onto your coats. Let's see what we can do here." Sounds like an auction coming up.

The elderly woman clings to her coat as though it were a child of hers. I could almost hear her whispering to herself, "Maybe they'll let me keep it or I might never see it again." Satisfied, the flight attendant disappears with her bags and begins looking for a place to stuff them. The woman watched anxiously as the man with her, a movie star look-alike, contents himself with fiddling with his pen, looking at it as though he had never seen one before. A new Mont Blanc with its shiny cap, the pen holds his complete and undivided attention.

"Is that another bag?" The flight attendant, back again for another inspection, is a bit firmer this time, believing they have somehow tried to hide a bag from him. The elderly couple reacts as though the flight attendant is about to mug them and take their carry-on luggage. The concern is written all over their faces. If you're not booked in First Class, it's part of the trauma of traveling with carry-ons.

I'd been on too many flights this year, but none of them had prepared me for Mr. Baby and the characters on this flight. True, they were mainly the same types of business personnel carrying their suit bags, their rolling carry-ons, and their computer cases. Pretty much the same, but there was a sprinkling of others. This flight, to LA, had to be different. Of course, it did. Who would call a child by something other than his name if not an LA mother?

Ok, I'm being unfair to LA mothers, but too many of them care more about looking good than caring for their kids. Bash me if you wish; I'm used to it. Thirty years in the field of psychology, and I've been called a lot of things. I've been burned by lit cigarettes when I tried to intercept a call to Alaska on the house phone of a mental health center. Once, I was warned that the woman I was with could "kill you fifty ways" as we sat in a hospital kitchen area. I didn't doubt her creativity because I knew she'd already killed one man and had almost done away with her psychiatrist. Well, gossip was that he did try to sexually molest her. But he was in a wheelchair. Did he deserve death? Not my call, please.

Free from the menacing world of institutional mental health, I was headed to California for a much-needed vacation among those with low humility. At least they wouldn't threaten to kill me fifty different ways; they'd only think it as they dawdled over their dirty martinis or whatever the drink of the moment was. Smiling faces can hide so much; it's amazing. When acting is your business, or you've inhaled so much of the entertainment industry, it's quite natural to smile and not mean it. Did any of them know about the Duchenne smile? Probably not.

All I knew was I was off, and it would be a world away from the gray, poorly lit small spaces where people lingered in pharmacologic stupors. It would be a great escape for sure, no motorcycle involved.

No, I would not be bringing anything more than jeans, shorts, tees, and personal care products, so I'd be traveling light. After all, this was a vacation, not an audition. Yes, I have gone to auditions, and they are horrid experiences where frightened people sit around and try to look confident even when they know they'll probably not get the gig.

In this plane's First Class, partially seen through the hanging curtain dividing "them" from "us," I see an overstuffed young man leaning back in his leather seat. He takes the glass of orange juice the flight attendant offers and drinks it down in one gulp. The seats are arranged two to a row, and the young man fills his seat completely. His ample belly hangs down over his waistband. The Turnbull & Asser shirt struggles to maintain the cascade of flesh beneath it while the Tiffany silver buckle on the belt struggles to do its share in the battle.

Meanwhile, in Economy, or whatever class they are calling it these days, the cabin crew attempts to maintain order with passengers who are already grumbling.

Flight attendants scratch their heads. Have you noticed? They also blow their noses while serving food. Why does this remind me of Edith Wharton's The Age of Innocence? What makes that line stand out, the one about not using anything other than a silver knife for cutting cucumbers? I don't know.

"Mr. Baby's tired, isn't he?" The voice of the young mother sounds sympathetic, but I feel Mr. Baby must surely be a toy. Perhaps he's some dream of a toy manufacturer's fantasy. This toy, the perfect baby, would cry, wet, and, possibly, vomit on command. But, please, not all over the Donna Karan suit mommy is wearing.

The cry sounds real. Was I out of touch with the world of toys and the genius of Mattel? It has to be a baby. But who would call an infant, "Mr. Baby?" Have we become that removed, that refined, that cultured, that even a baby, little Marys and Roberts, and Charlies and Harrys, are now Mr. and Ms. Baby? Oh, well—this plane was headed for the West Coast, and she was a California mother.

The flight seemed uneventful except for Mr. Baby, who was crying uncontrollably and kicking. I accepted the headset the flight attendant offered to me, even though I had no interest in the film, but perhaps it would muffle Mr. Baby and his incessant screams. California mommy looks at the headset as though it had cooties. But, on this plane, it was free, so she took it with two fingers, wiped it with a disinfectant towelette from her purse, and sat back.

I was bored, and I began to give my imagination free rein. What are those insistent "pings" that ring on airplanes? Have you ever wondered? Is the captain telling the crew that they will have to abandon ship or that he has to go to the powder room or wants the flight attendant to prepare for landing? Is he telling the crew he wants more coffee or he forgot where he's supposed to be landing today?

Do they have a series of "secret" codes that would let us in on all manner of stupid things, if we only had the knowledge? I was tired of all this secret communication, of Mr. Baby and his crying, the dinky little snacks and the people moving their capacious hips into my space in these things they call seats.

Who is that "average passenger" they use to decide the width of these seats? Is it that "average woman" for whom they make all those size 8s or 10s, 12s and 14s? I never fit into any of them, seats included. Then, of course, there is that store that makes size 2–3s. I told the saleswoman I must have stopped in the wrong store. "No, dear, believe me, you are a size 3." Well, I'm not, but who's arguing when they drop your blouse size by 10?

I wanted to fling off my seat belt, in apparent violation of the lighted sign, run up into First Class, and demand to use their restroom. Have you ever noticed how they guard that restroom? Even when no one is using it and the conveniences in the Economy section are full, they still won't let you use it.

So, for something like $2,000, I could buy the right to a WC reserved expressly for the anointed. One wonders about the elegant tushes that linger there. Was there something special about that restroom, too?

Oh, I was in fine form. I would refuse to take my seat in Economy, I would demand decent meals, and put my seat into the fully reclined, not upright, position. Who cares if I would be lying almost face up in the lap of the passenger behind me?

I wanted freedom on this flight, but, of course, the voice of Sister Irenita Marie called out loud and clear: "Stop being a bold, fresh piece." I stopped my fantasy dead in its tracks. Sister was right; I would behave.

Mr. Baby continued to cry fitfully until he exhausted himself or was filled to the epiglottis with all that milk his mother was dutifully pressing on him. A loud roar was reduced to sobs and then to soft little moans and then, finally, silence.

Was Mr. Baby asleep in a milk-induced stupor, or had his mother drugged him? Who knew? He was quiet for the rest of the flight, and I stopped allowing the beast inside my head to run rampant with my senses.

I quieted down, too. I busied myself with scrutinizing the elaborate flight patterns on the back of the safety instructions, which I had pulled from the seat pocket. In the in-flight merchandise magazine, I looked dutifully at all the "wonderful" things I could squander my every cent on.

I wondered if these items were indeed only for "in-flight purchase," or could anyone, who hadn't had their sanity taxed by Mr. Baby, buy them while on the ground? Was this an actual reward for what I'd just suffered through? No, anyone could buy them. No exclusivity here.

Hopes dashed, I listened to the captain drone on about what we could see if there weren't so many clouds in our way, and how we could expect to be landing "shortly."

I know that most of us would think of "shortly" as meaning that something would happen within a specific length of time. In airline lingo, however, it means whatever it means.

Airline lingo is similar to how we think about IQ tests. When someone asks what an IQ test measures, we dutifully answer, "An IQ test measures whatever an IQ test measures," and hope that they won't take us away in a clean white jacket complete with lovely buckles down the back.

Yes, I'm a psychologist. Still, even psychologists have their limits and, no, we don't sit passively while patients call us all sorts of names.

Inside, those of us who have blood coursing through our veins may even fantasize about seizing the opportunity to let our patients find someone else or suggesting that they might like a referral to someone else.

Of course, that means less income. Still, I've always thought that my mental health is important, too, and income cannot compensate me for tolerating the boorish behavior of people who think I'm a paid whipping girl.

The plane landed, and I learned that "shortly" actually meant twenty minutes on this flight. I grabbed my bag from the overhead, trotted off the plane, and left Mr. Baby and all my fellow passengers to their own devices. It was pleasant to feel the sting of the Los Angeles air in my eyes.

One thing I knew: I'd be back, and who knew what adventures awaited me on that return flight? I could only hope that Mr. Baby was home to stay in LA.

A TIGER'S TALE

The dull pain in her thigh was a reminder. It would always be so, and the memory of that grilling at the hospital would never leave the child's memory portion of her brain. Today, the hospital memory came back for another go-round of trauma and an adult understanding of those who eagerly look for things that aren't there.

In the hospital emergency room, a woman is standing over her. The air smells of familiar antiseptics that assail the little girl's nostrils. Looking too large for any human head, the woman's face, surrounded by a rough halo of curly hair, comes within inches of her nose. Anger and authority are written all over her face. The social worker wants to have her way and the evidence she seeks.

It doesn't matter that the surgeon is waiting to perform emergency surgery; she will have her admission of guilt. They're about to wheel the gurney to the operating room elevator, and she needs to get her evidence now. The social worker requires an entry of responsibility into her notes, and time is short.

"Tell me," she insists in a breath smelling of cigarettes and coffee. The noxious odors are unpleasant and alien to the little girl.

The light hurts the girl's eyes as the lamp flashes behind the woman's moving head. The green-tiled room is hot, and her leg is throbbing with pain. Her parents are outside, her father holding back the tears he so wants to free.

"They hurt you, didn't they?" the woman continues with an increased intensity bordering on a command as the medical staff rushes to prepare for the emergency surgery.

"They burned you, and that's how you got that wound! Didn't your parents burn you?" The grilling continues in blatant disregard for the surgical sheets, the pole for the IV, and the scurrying staff rushing to hold the elevator.

"Tell me what they did to you!" It was a command, almost a scream, in a tone the girl had never heard. But the woman cannot recognize the six-year-olds absence of fear of anyone or anything.

A child, a frail young tiger in a family of stoics, who challenges herself in feats other children avoid, knows she is right. The thought strengthens her resolve to respond to this agitated woman. And the words of her sister come to her.

Her older sister had said, "You remember when mommy and daddy were making believe they were fighting? Only three years old, and you picked up a coat hanger and ran at daddy yelling, 'You stop! You can't hurt my mommy.'"

Now, she would stand up again, but this time she is three years older, and the young tiger is more robust than before.

"They didn't hurt me! They did what the doctor told them to do, and they took me home. They didn't hurt me!" She screws up her face in defiance. Small for her age, she nevertheless feels suited to the task.

Frustrated, the woman turns to the staff in the room. "I know they hurt her. I know she's a victim of child abuse, but she won't admit it because she's afraid." The comment implores others to pitch in on her interrogation, but all stare at her in poorly contained disbelief, casting their eyes downward. The only notice is the shuffling of feet and turning away as though busy with tasks.

A surgeon speaks in whispers to the girl's parents in one corner. "We don't know if we can save the leg. The decision to amputate, high near the hip, won't be made until we get in there and see what we can do. It's a chance, but I wanted to prepare you in case we have to amputate."

The father stares off at his daughter, who is talking to an overwrought, red-faced woman. Pulling her handkerchief from her pocket, the mother permits herself one low sob. Stoicism has always been her escape, and it has permeated her other children, but not this one, the last and smallest of her brood. The child she never wanted and tried to abort faces a life of disability. Was this the mother's punishment?

The charity clinic obstetricians told her she would have twins, unthinkable in a family already in dire need of money to survive. "Do you want to keep this pregnancy?" he asked with some hesitation. How could she tell him she didn't want this child?

Unable to say the words, a slow head movement showed she didn't want the pregnancy to continue. The physician provides an injection to cause a miscarriage. Her husband would never know, and it would appear natural. But this one baby tiger refuses, hangs on to life, and is born.

Good health didn't follow. The child had already survived two episodes of pneumonia, one two years ago. She was the sickly child in the family. Would she survive this?

"If you have to amputate," the mother asks as she finds her voice. "Will she have an artificial leg?"

"No," the surgeon responds with a note of resignation. "It will be too high up for that."

"How will she get around?" Even the thought brought an involuntary shiver to her spine.

Looking at the mother as he shoves his hands into his pocket, his answer is anything but reassuring. "She'll always have to use crutches and a wheelchair."

The staff is whirling around the room now, seeming to rush, and there are the faint clinking sounds of metal-on-metal as trays clash. In the distance, an elevator hums and jars to a stop as the massive door slides open widely. There are two main stops for this service elevator with a door in front and back: the operating room and the morgue.

Out of the corner of her eye, the mother sees the nurses in white outfits standing, changing their weight from one foot to the other. An air of impatience pervades the room.

The vision of her little girl and her nearly impossible task of mounting the house's front steps and then the flight of stairs to the second-floor cold-water flat is almost too much, but the mother maintains her calm appearance. She doesn't want to frighten her daughter, who might have a disability. Crippled. The word is unthinkable.

The surgical team propels the gurney with sheets flying toward the waiting elevator, giving little regard for the children's services woman. Somehow, they know she wishes to file a criminal complaint against the little girl's parents.

The child knows where she is going, her prior illness has acquainted her with hospital procedures. But she doesn't know they might have to amputate her leg, the reason her father has tears running down his rugged face now.

A nurse moves the parents quickly to a waiting room where one window affords a view of the elevator, and they watch as the table disappears into the elevator car and the door shuts abruptly with a thud. It is a sound that carries with it a sense of something ominous.

"Promise you'll wake me when it's over," the girl asks a nurse. "We will," the woman responds. How does she even know to ask that question?

In the emergency room, the social worker seethes with anger. An elderly physician, who knows the family and has reviewed the girl's chart, approaches the woman. The deep lines on his forehead appear deeper as he prepares to speak to her.

"Your zeal is admirable," he begins, "but the intern who saw them initially told them to go home and apply hot compresses, as hot as she could bear. She only had a sizeable puffy swelling on her leg. He didn't know she had a torn vein in her leg."

"They followed his instructions and applied the hot compresses until the swelling continued to grow into something that frightened them. Then they brought their daughter back to the hospital. There was no child abuse. They love that little girl, and you wanted to brand them, abusers? I think you need to go home and think that over."

The physician turns and walks away, sighing, leaving the woman looking around as the rest of the staff drifts off.

Years later, there would be charges against the social worker from the emergency room for filing false complaints of child abuse. They would find her guilty of abuse of her authority and she would leave her job. No one knew where she went, but there was a rumor of suicide.

The little girl's protests to support her parents would be vindicated, but she would never know as she closed the two buckles on her new pair of skates.

THE BANKER

The morning air is heavy with the sticky heat of summer. The window shades refuse to move, not refusing but unable, crippled. Not a single breeze. Quiet gloom, hot. Sweat is the sole relief.

Stealthily, she moves as a thief toward the dresser. A white envelope stands out in its starkness in the heavy wooden drawer as she slowly opens it. The envelope lies atop the carefully tatted, gifted hankies and the half-empty box of Fatima cigarettes.

On the envelope's front, in clear, unmistakable penciled Palmer script, are the words, Don't Touch.

An emotional shock jolts her as she hesitates while the blankets behind her rise and fall in a slow rhythm. The years have been ones of never refusing an order, never asking, "Why?"

She knows she is now about to disobey the rules by which she was raised. Her heart is beating faster. The sweat beads transform into small rivulets on her face.

She must push the penciled mandate out of her mind. Years of unquestioning acceptance are willfully erased with force from her mind. She slips the envelope open carefully, not knowing what to expect.

Inside, ten slightly crumpled hundred-dollar bills. Where did she get this money and why was it to be left untouched?

Unexpectedly, the familiar yet feeble voice behind her asks, "What are you doing?" Riveted in place, she is stunned, and, in a panic, freezes, her hand still on the bills. The voice fades. The medications are working.

Was this what her sister was talking about? Their mother was holding money for a neighbor's funeral expenses. Mary, the indigent neighbor diagnosed with a fatal illness, hid her money until she found a "banker" whom she could trust, someone who would never reveal her secret.

The envelope is her burial money, now safe in an old, wooden second-hand dresser in her dying mother's bedroom. It must not be touched but kept until needed when the neighbor's family will know to call for it.

Emotion is a black pit in her stomach. How empty she feels. Months of suffering and nights of watching life slip away have eroded all feelings. What is left is a yearning for it to be over for everyone, but primarily for her mother, who was always there for anyone who needed her. Now, her mother needs her in a way that most may find unacceptable; she wants her mother to die.

Only an hour ago, she was making what some dark humorist might call her drug run. So clear in her mind, she could pull it all back now.

The car is slowly moving along, creeping. On the dashboard a rusty tire iron lays, waiting and serving as a signal, a warning. Keeping a distance that allows for a quick turn, she drives with resolve.

A small red canvas bag has two carefully wrapped brown bottles containing the precious liquid. She must protect it. People would kill to get it. She knows this like she knows a mother will protect an infant. Now, she is protecting her mother. She clutches the wheel tighter and stares straight ahead, neither looking right nor left. There must be no sign of weakness or wonder should anyone be watching. It's important to look strong, tough.

With a prayer for protection, there is also one for death, a release from pain, and from a life of emotional twists. Not for herself, but for the person awaiting her delivery.

The delivery is made, the extra-strong potion prepared and soon there will be relief in a coma that pushes all sounds into the darkness of eternal sleep. It won't be long now. The nurse has come and called an ambulance. The hospital room awaits. The ambulance leaves in haste, as though on an emergency call, but this is no emergency. It is the last car trip her mother will make alive.

Hospitals are formidable fortresses that promise relief and life, but today a group of daughters assembles for a different kind of relief; one that promises an end, not a continuance of life. Silently, the women are led to a small room outside the nursing station. It is the room assigned to those who are dying and require immediate attention for their final moments.

The circle of quiet women, almost like strangers, without a word or a touch between them, gathers; all eyes are on the woman in the bed. The chest moves almost imperceptibly with low, rumbling sounds signaling life, but only barely. The next deed will have to be done as quietly as breathing.

"She's got pneumonia. Do you want me to treat it?" The young physician looks at the women for an answer and one signals nothing is to be done. No words, no muffled discussion, nothing, and it is done.

"All right, then, I'll make her comfortable." The unnerving, silent soundless needle is pushed into the IV tubing but hits everyone's ears as loud as a drumbeat.

The physician moves silently out of the room as though by magic. She vaporizes down the hall in the shafts of very early morning light. Barely a hint of dawn is showing as the floor-to-ceiling diaphanous curtains lift in a bowing gesture as she passes.

Minutes seem like hours as they watch silently. Not a move, not a word. All eyes are on the bed where the raising of the chest slows until it stops.

One eye is closed, but one remains starkly open, staring straight at the daughter who is the red-bag courier. The light hazel orb continues the fixed stare. The task of holding the thousand dollars for the burial of the neighbor has been passed.

A nurse glides into the room, extends a steady hand, one finger outstretched, and brings the open eyelid down. A cool breeze stirs the warm room.

A mist is sweeping over the bed. Or is it a figment of imagination? Out the doorway it trails down the hall past the curtains that fly up, French doors opening and shutting suddenly. In moments it passes, the curtains fall back against the panes, but the courier feels a coolness in her nostrils, filling her lungs.

The others seem unmoved, as though they saw nothing. The sweat glistens on their brows as they sit like statues.

But from somewhere in the hollows of her soul, the red-bag courier feels the stirring of life as an unmistakable keening begins. Her throat refuses to contain it. Unnerved, the women glimpse at her momentarily, shuffle a bit and return to stiffness once again. Then, all is quiet.

But the red-bag courier knows she is the banker now.

THE COMMUNION DRESS

The rain pounded on the roof while the sickening smell of the flowers in his nostrils added to the lump in his throat. Knowing what he was about to do gnawed at him as a tearful haze clouded his eyes. All so vivid, it could have been yesterday.

The weight of the hammer in his hand, a smooth handle with a heavy head would do it. He brought it down smartly to drive the merciless nails into the wooden lid of the coffin.

In his mind, he knew she was being tossed with each strike and his muscles rebelled, but he persisted. The hammer slipped in his calloused hand, almost falling to the floor. He renewed his resolve.

His grip now whitened his knuckles; he was the father, and it was his duty to ensure her safe journey to the grave.

A flush of heat sent beads of sweat across his furrowed brow, creating a crown-like glow. The bedcovers intensify his internal heat, and he begins to push them off.

It was then that he noticed her in this room decorated with fading roses wallpaper, old bits of furniture, worn shoes thrown under a bureau, and a seaman's cap on the bedpost.

"Mary, Mary dear, what are you doing here?" A wizened man in his rumpled sheets is looking at his small daughter standing at the foot of his bed. In her pale hand, she is holding something, but in the flashes of light and darkness from the streetlight, it's unclear.

The streetlight flickers outside, creating patterns of light and shadow in the room. He doesn't want to complain to the electric company about the loose corrugated metal plate protecting the fragile bulb.

He doesn't want to make trouble. In this stage of life, he knows making trouble can be a problem. When he was younger, he'd speak up, shout and even threaten to get his way, but not now. The fight had gone out of him after the accident. Who listens to a man with one leg?

He is tired as anyone can be after losing a child, and here it is decades later, the anniversary. The thought of the ground that day, so cold and wet, sends shivers down his spine. All of them looked away when he approached the ugly hole. What were they thinking? He knew. Her death was caused by him.

The shoes he wore that day with the flaking mud on them are in his mind, where they have settled into a kind of permanence, like a scar.

The shoes, the shoes! They said he'd brought mud into the house. Fever followed as quickly as a hot storm that swallowed her, and she was gone.

Through his brain fog he remembers the white roses and the glistening drops of rain like tiny diamonds. The roses lay on the casket as it was lowered into the black hole.

The man's granddaughter in the next room is on the phone. Her feelings of loyalty to the family cause hesitancy even as she saw his rapid decline in the last few weeks. If only she had someone to help, she'd get the advice that would make it all right and ease the guilt. But there is no one.

Slowly, her finger pokes out the phone number. Each digit pressed makes it worse. She wants to cry, but she mustn't alert him to what she's thinking. Finally, the phone is answered, and her voice falters.

"Doctor, I think he's getting worse. Yes, we may have to consider putting him someplace safer than our home."

"What's happened that made you change your mind?"

Again, she hesitates, but she knows he's the only help she has.

"We both know how he's been acting lately since my husband died from that fever. I even hid his straight razor. I never knew he could be so gruff, so unhappy, and so tearful. He's never been a man who cries. Now, if he can't find his slippers, he cries. Imagine that? Today, he claims he saw his dead little daughter, my father's youngest sister, who died many years ago, standing at the foot of his bed. He even described the dress she was wearing, which was her First Holy Communion dress. It was the one for her funeral. I saw it because someone took a photo of her in the casket."

The answer comes back in an assuring tone. "Well, if he's beginning to see things, yes, that may mean more brain damage from that tile floor. I know he's been unsteady on his leg. We'll begin the process of placement. I do have somewhere in mind. I'll ask to have a bed reserved for him. Do you think he'll agree?"

The decision causes her head to throb. "I don't know. He's always been so independent, and now I'm worrying. We're alone in the house most of the time, and when he's not crying, he's so angry."

The woman puts down the phone, dejected, and begins walking softly toward the bedroom. The old man, bent over, has returned to his bed's sheets. Lying motionless under the heavy blankets that push against the thick, white stubble on his chin, his mouth is drooping on one side. The gray eyes are fixed, staring at the foot of the bed.

The woman looks down, and there, lying on the bed is a rain-bejeweled fresh white rose.

SHE SLEEPS

"Where..." the question trails off from lips that refuse to form the words.

"She's in the trunk."

"Oh, I didn't know."

Ahead lays the small storm-torn inlet leading to where the boat is anchored. Now the bridge is stuck and isn't releasing and locks in the open position with a thud. It reaches up skyward as we watch.

I want to jump out of the car and force the bridge down or yell at the man in the control booth to make it come down. A hand reaches over to mine, and a look tells me to sit and wait.

"We're stuck here until they fix it." The car engine is turned off. Everyone sits and waits in uncomfortable silence, but a sigh signals the wait is welcomed.

Wind is kicking up. Is that a laugh? Did I hear her laugh, or is my mind wishing it were so? No, I'd know that throaty laugh anywhere. It's her.

She knows, and she's playing a last joke on us with the bridge. We wait. I hear no more laughter. The groan of gears signals the bridge is falling into position. Just then, though, a bit of a laugh. Now she's done with us, and we can go on our way to the boat?

But the engine struggles to catch. The driver tries again and again, but it won't start, and I wonder why this is happening. She doesn't want us to leave. She's hanging onto us.

We can't stay. The boat is waiting for us.

Finally, after what seems like hours but must be only anxious minutes, the engine coughs, and the car jerks and moves forward at a snail's pace over the bridge. Even the car seems to hold us back.

Now the parking lot is in sight, and the car is guided to an empty spot.

The dock rocks, and water splashes through the slats as our group boards. She is plucked from the trunk and carried in a shopping bag, placed near the boat ladder where she waits. It won't be long now.

Thornless roses are handed out as the boat slips through the dark waters past the bobbing bait shack with the sign, Anglers, Fresh Bait Here. The salt air isn't refreshing. Nothing is as usual.

Snacks and beers don't burden a side table. The beers almost evaporate. Little regard is given to snacks. Alcohol is what we need, not nuts or pretzels.

A call to assemble. A short prayer. The dissolvable white container is retrieved from the shopping bag and lovingly slipped into the water to settle among the seashells and the bay grasses. Quietly and noiselessly, its whiteness fades from sight as we watch and toss our flowers into the water. How can this be our last goodbye?

Do I hear a cat? There are no cats on this desolate spit of sand in the bay. There are no animals. Then I remember. Her cats were to stay with her.

Now she sleeps in her happy place where she once fished, and we are left to mourn and clear out her house.

HARD WORK

Hard work makes a hot shower that much more pleasant. The water slides over his body, the suds run effortlessly down his legs and arms. A delight. His hairy skin plays tug-of-war with the towel. The end of hard work is the pleasure enjoyed now that it's done.

Some days are better than others, and this one, admittedly, was one of the best. He carefully laid out the clothing. Looking down now at the crisp white shirt, new tie, and the carefully ironed undershirt and shorts to see them lined up neatly, waiting on the dresser. The suit hung in front of the closet just as he had left it that morning. Preparation was important.

Today was to be different. The rough push on the bed by his mother's knee shook him awake suddenly; her voice was gravel in his ears. But today, he had a different day in mind, a day that would be that hard day's work.

The yelling from the kitchen continued as it had in the bedroom, but it didn't cut as before; he was now immune to the crunching sounds as he went about his tasks. First, a bowl of cold cereal, a cup of her strong coffee, and a bit of silent reflection. Today was his day, not her's, as it always had been.

The old-fashioned bed she refused to replace was perfect. The mattress was tossed, and the wooden slats, thick and robust, pulled out easily. They didn't have rounded edges, which was hard on the hands.

The old memory of a baby brother lying in a crib came to mind. It would be like that. A sharpened pencil hadn't done the job. The closet was a safe place then, but today he wouldn't hide.

A trip to the hospital, stitches, and antibiotics, and the baby lived for how many more years before he had that accident. Those cellar steps were so dangerous. Each time he had to walk down them, he felt like he was descending into a black hole with nothing to hold on to.

It had been the day he asked if he could have money to buy some candy and his favorite horror and superhero comic books. He read in a stumbling fashion. Anyone with an IQ below 70 had problems, but he loved the artwork, the colors, the bulging muscles, and the swift action. Reading gave him a sense of being one of those superheroes, even with his thick glasses and awkward gait.

A loud screech bounced off the shiny, painted kitchen walls.

"Look, you've scared Peaches. Now, now, baby, mommy is going to give you a nice big cracker, and then you can take a bath. Would you like that, darlin'?" She leaned over and stroked the bird's head, almost caressing it as though it were a child she loved. He watched as he stood in the doorway. The sight was added motivation for his job.

Always penny-pinching, never allowing him any small pleasures or bits of candy.

"You want candy! All it does is rot your teeth, and I'm not paying for a dentist. Get that idea out of your head, young man."

"Candy! Where do you think all this money comes from? What do you do all day long? I go out and do hard work. Hard work, you hear me? Don't sit around, washing my hands all day long. I do hard work! Why didn't you go back to that workshop? Then you'd have money for candy."

Sponges on cardboard was a job that didn't require looking up. But two years was a slice of his life for pennies. One day, he lashed out, and the incident cost him. He was fired and couldn't go back. She knew it.

"Nonsense, you spend my hard-earned money on. Look at this nonsense, nonsense, nonsense!"

Roughly, she tore The Hulk and Batman, and Tomb of Dracula in fours and threw them into the large trash can outside the kitchen door. Slamming the cover on the galvanized steel, she looked up at him with an ugly sneer on her face. His muscles tensed. But that wasn't today.

The sounds of her yelling echoed in his ears as if he could hear her, but of course, he couldn't.

Done. Finally done. The bird was the problem, with its squawking and all those feathers flying. But that was quickly done, too. No more squawking, ever. Kick it out of the way. Must get dressed now and take another shower. Sweat more than he had planned.

Looking down at his hands, he noticed they weren't clean.

It's so sticky. And it just doesn't come off easily, and you have to be so careful that you don't get it on your clothes. No one wants to see somebody in stained clothes.

His thoughts were moving fast. Even in swinging, he was careful. It never hit him, just the walls. Why are feathers so sticky? Those damn things are all between his fingers.

The house is quiet. Not a sound except for the creak of the occasional floorboard under his foot as he walks into the kitchen to the door where he stands at the top of the cellar stairs looking. It's dark, but he can see just a bit of the apron and a foot turned in an odd direction. A single potholder lay near the cellar door. Now the light was changing as early evening brought a shadow pattern on the linoleum floor.

Enough. Time to get dressed. The phone call had already been made, and they'd be there soon.

A SUNNY DAY

Afternoon sun drills through the air, the ground, and the garden surrounding the house. The day screams out for air conditioning and the tinted windows of the car tightly hold in the cool, artificial breeze flowing over her.

He appears rushing from the front door to the garage when a screech, a roar, flying pebbles and he flips onto the gravel. A quick turn, a push into reverse, and a bump raises the car momentarily.

The cell phone makes indistinct noises as she punches the three numbers. *"Operator, I'd like to report an accident."*

ONCE UPON A TRADITION

Tradition binds us together, much like an invisible, social glue that secures our worlds and keeps them from flying out of kilter. When tradition meets resistance, which may have built up over time, the result is often unpleasant.

Maxwell knows what he must do, and he knows what is expected of him, but the very thought brings burning moisture up into his throat. He wants to vomit and run away, but he can't. The reason? Tradition's glue holds him fast. He must stand firm right now. Everyone around him expects he will fulfill the duty tradition has laid upon his young, fragile shoulders. Today, he must be a man and do what men in families do.

Lacking a blue suit, in fact, any suit makes the experience even more uncomfortable as he moves around inside his white shirt as though his feelings brought out an invisible rash. It's upsetting. He is shockingly improperly garbed, standing here among men who wear suits as part of their job.

The men decide he is to be given a pass since it is his father who lies in the poorly stained wooden casket. Who but a family that could only afford this final insignificant vehicle of passage to the everlasting unknown sends a boy dressed like this? Not their problem, but his is the unspoken decision as they stand by waiting for the task's completion.

As the boy is wobbling in the sickening smell of the flowers decorating the room, his thoughts go back to those searing dinner table experiences, and the words bounce around in his head like handballs. The anger is welling up and setting his blood pressure to a point where his head is aching. But the men see nothing but a dutiful son, not one who wants this to be over before he runs away.

How many meals has he pushed down his throat as he heard that familiar rant that never stopped, but it will never fill the room like a hateful verbal stench anymore?

"*You'll be pushing up daisies before me!*" his father yells. The anger is undeserved but ever-present. He is the only boy in the family and the target of his father's enmity for a life not well lived.

An additional unfortunate event was his being named after a car his father was refurbishing and which caused a significant injury. The car would provide them passage into the middle class, but that dream crashed into oblivion as the motor braces gave way.

Unexpectedly, the father's life plans are fading like old wallpaper. Ruined dreams haunt his mind as the never-ending torturing pain he cannot staunch with bottles of sickeningly sweet rock-and-rye whiskey. The rock candy rattling in the bottle promises something it cannot deliver, but he tries to believe the lie, anyway.

"*Yeah,*" Maxwell yells back, attempting a futile response to the most recent blast, "*you'll be there before me!*" Inside he is tensing his muscles and hoping tears never well up in his eyes. That would be a victory for the brute he calls father.

His mother sits silent, as do his three sisters, who fear that any move may re-direct them into this spotlight of hot anger. One of Maxwell's sisters, however, foolishly breaks out with giggles and begins talking about a school chum's mistakes in class that day. It is an error she is about to regret.

Suddenly rising from her seat, the chair banging as it lands on the floor, the mother grabs a large carving knife from the table and throws it at the girl. Failing precision, the blade narrowly misses the girl's eye, slicing through her fair skin, and splitting it in a gash. A thin, red line wiggles down her face. Next, a red blotch spreads like a web over her dress. Giggles turn to terror as she screams and cries.

"*Now look what you've done,*" the father yells at Maxwell. How is he to blame for his mother's act of violence toward his sister? It doesn't matter. He is blamed for everything, whether responsible or not. And he's rarely responsible for the constant barrage of abuse.

"*I did nothing,*" he pleads.

"*Shut up and get me the bandage and tape from the kitchen,*" he is commanded.

The mother sits in silence, not attempting to quell the bleeding wound as the father presses it shut.

That day, it was both verbal and physical violence from both parents. Why was he born in the first place? It is a question that could, if answered honestly, provide a clue to the reason for the torrent of verbal abuse.

But the time of retribution has come as one of the suited men hands an odd hammer to Maxwell. Without hesitation, he grasps it firmly, his fingers placed to ensure a good grip.

"*Ok, kid, now you drive the nail in here,*" the man directs as he points to one slender spike placed into the lid of the coffin. The rest of the nail's journey will be Maxwell's job. He thought he would relish it, but his stomach is churning.

Swiftly, thoughtlessly, he slams the hammer down at the nail as though it were an enemy in battle. The enemy, in fact, is being sealed forever inside the box, and Maxwell will have his revenge. Done. It is done and the men direct him to leave as they remove the remains to the waiting hearse.

When would the daisies begin pushing up? He couldn't help the black thought, the gut-twisting anger that comes over him as he slowly walks away from the rent in the earth that is quietly being filled. The sound of pebbles bouncing off the coffin is strange, reassuring music. Maxwell's ears welcome it.

It is over, but is it?

DIAMOND EARRINGS FOR BABY

Baby's small fingers with their glistening red nails are toying with the one-carat diamond earrings in her pierced ears. Her moment of triumph will be realized when she is on the TV show later today.

Her mother and a family friend sit on the tufted settee in the hotel room.

"You know," the weary friend says, "it sure was a stroke of luck that other little girl lost her flipper. That gap in her front teeth stood out to the judges like a bonfire in a snowstorm. Baby sure was lucky that day, like the time that little boy got so sick he had to be taken home."

"It wasn't luck," Baby screeches, standing with arms akimbo, her face pinched up like a paper bag filled with air. "He drank too much lemonade. It was all his fault." Fire fairly flames from her eyes at her mother daring her to say anything. "Now, where's my dress I'm going to wear on TV today? You didn't forget it, did you?"

Slender young arms raise like threatening yard sticks prepared to render their punishment. An index finger points directly at her mother as Baby demands, "Where is my dress?"

Flustered, the mother manages a tepid response. "I packed it. I know I packed it carefully. It's got to be here."

The room is a blizzard of activity as the women scurry around, pulling open suitcases and closets, but the dress is nowhere.

Furious that they left the dress behind, Baby races to the bathroom. Effortlessly, she lands on the windowsill and throws the window open. Twelve stories below, the traffic is building. No window guards, no bars, and no locks spoil the view. Baby's silhouette is a live figure in a new frieze.

"I'll jump if you don't find that dress," she screams, turning her head toward her mother and the mother's friend. Her face is contorted as the blood rushes up to her head, forcing veins to line her temples.

The women plead for Baby to come down. They'll do something, anything, to get her a dress for the show.

Just then, a knock on the door. A bellman returns the dress he discovered in the bellman's closet. Seeing Baby wobbling in the wide-open window, without a second thought, he rushes into the bathroom, clutches Baby's small waist, and pulls her into the room.

Forcing his eyes to remain fixed on Baby and tensing his mouth to calm himself, the bellman manages a short response. "Oh," he stutters, "I forgot. There's this message left at the front desk." The note is passed to the mother.

The note is brief but to the point.

Baby's appearance was a soft booking. She's being replaced by a plant lady. The big moment Baby envisioned won't be coming in the future, either; a growth spurt and facial pimples will see to that.

THE LAST SWIM

The blue water reflecting the sunlight in flashes of light is inviting. All around the pool, the gardeners trim away trees to create an open patch for the sun to warm the shimmering water. Swimming is her favorite exercise.

Mara is lying in her bright bikini bathing suit on a chaise off to the side, not quite in the shade and still in full sun. Ole sole's work paints a chamois color on her taut dancer's body. The ballerina wants to be in this sunshine, and they read her mind to provide all she wishes. It will always be that way now. Echoes from the past still fill the void around the pool.

"I want to dance! I want to be a ballerina and wear beautiful outfits!" How many times did her mother hear those two sentences? The family provides the esteemed school and the former prima donna for private lessons. The lessons go well, and Mara is almost ready for her first dance in the hallowed hall they contracted for her troupe. But there remained one thing that stands in her way.

Eighteen and ready for the stage, the young dancer wants nothing to interfere with her desires and career plans. She wants a hysterectomy to end the monthly pain and banish the possibility of pregnancy. No, children are not in Mara's plans, and her parents, somewhat distressed, agree. Only children often get their way.

The physician concludes the pain will always be there. Only drugs will stop it, but that would mean she couldn't dance for a week or more.

"Before I go for the surgery, let me get in one last swim." She scrunches up her shoulders, giggling, looking down at her flat stomach, knowing it will always be that way, and plunges into the deep, dark-blue end of the pool.

Surgery is swift and without incident and she lies in bed in the dim evening light with no one noticing anything unusual. Nurses, interns, and her physician all find her doing well, if a bit more than groggy. The numbers on the monitor flutter but yell no emergencies. It is the usual after-surgery, low blood pressure handled with bags of fluids.

A night nurse is the first to sound a shrieking alarm as she checks Mara's bed, now soaked with the precious fluid of life. Frantic efforts fail to defeat the coma that seizes her body but doesn't result in death. "My God, she's bleeding out," the head nurse yells.

Afterward, weeks of consultation, charges of malpractice and a lawsuit do nothing to lift the coma.

"It's irreversible," their family physician announces. Did they want her sent to live out the rest of her life in a rehab facility? He rattled some of the best in the country off, one by one.

"No," her mother screams, her face contorted in an unusual mass of furrows. "We're taking her home. She'll have nurses day and night. It's where she belongs, where she wants to be. I want her to be home when she wakes up." That was months ago.

They set up a virtual outpatient clinic in the home. Every medical need will be met, and everyone waits for the fateful day of awakening. The air fills with statements that reinforce the mother's belief. In private, the staff, like the family physician, has a different view.

Today, they massage her with luxuriant suntan lotion to ensure an even tan. Tomorrow, they will dress her in something fashionable and rest her in the shade. If it rains, they will settle her on the sofa in the music room where her ballet slippers hang. She's home.

Finished with the suntan lotion, the nurse rushes from the pool toward the house and brushes into a table holding a metal tray. Now, a loud clanging noise pierces the air as the tray hits the pool's stone decking. The day nurse puts the tray back on the table and continues toward the door. She knows the night nurse is waiting and will take over.

A slight twitch in response to the noise, an abrupt head movement, and a brief flutter of Mara's eyelids go unnoticed by the nurse, leaving quickly at the end of her shift. Whether the mother was right to bring her home for her awakening is no longer a question the staff considers.

But is her mother's love the medicine that Mara needs to come back to them? Tomorrow they may know.

HOSPITAL FLOWERS' ANGEL

The small metal cart with its gleaming trays was being wheeled rapidly down the hallway of the critical care unit of the hospital. On the top and bottom trays were vases full of colorful flowers that shook like enthusiastic fans going to a home game. But one peculiarity of the flowers stood out: they were a bit past their sell-by date. Some roses looked tired, with heads bent slightly forward.

Pushing the cart was a smiling, gray-haired woman wearing faux pearls and eyeglasses on a chain around her neck. As she walked, she glanced at each room, casually flashing a smile and a vigorous wave as she moved on.

Why would anybody be bringing flowers that were not fresh to a hospital? The thought barely flashed through the mind of a young worker walking down the hall. The worker, a female nursing assistant, stopped and, with an almost imperceptible frown on her face, made a half turn and looked over her shoulder at the cart speeding down the long hallway.

Stopping by the nursing station, the grey-haired woman pushing the cart flicked the pink smock that identified her as a volunteer. Stray bits of flowers or baby's breath were quickly dispatched. She was, after all, very concerned about her appearance and her outfit.

The nurse inquired which patients would get the flowers and when she would dispense them.

"Oh, I give them to the patients that are not doing well. As I place the flowers in their room, I tell them that if they would pray more, their illness could heal, and they really don't need modern medicine." In a hospital? The nursing supervisor, also seated at the desk, was puzzled.

The supervisor, finding this an unusual philosophy on a hospice unit, didn't think it was time to show she disagreed with the woman's approach. Better to allow her to go on distributing the flowers, but something needed to be done about what she was telling the patients.

It was almost punishment from this volunteer flower woman with the sunny appearance. And the nurse knew that last year, while the flower woman's husband was in the throes of a significant cardiac event, the woman encouraged him to pray more and not to call 911 immediately. Of course, that didn't go well, despite her imploring him on the phone to pray more. She blamed his lack of prayer. The burial, without a wake, was a day later. She never shed a tear.

But telling terminally ill patients we could heal them with prayer wasn't the extent of the flower woman's "helpful" activities. One week previously, the woman bragged to a nurse, "Yes, I had to drown the kittens I found in a box outside the apartment house. I did it in our guest bathroom. No one ever uses it. Who wants those flea-infested things ruining the neighborhood?" Deep scratches on her hands evidenced that this didn't go well, either.

Proud of her having acted on behalf of her neighbors, she would go to her weekly duties distributing flowers at the hospital. First, there was one stop she had to make in her shiny new SUV, the funeral home, for more flowers.

Today, the nursing supervisor could no longer ignore the concerns of the staff. This woman volunteer must stop what she was telling patients. "We're a place of care for the dying, not a religious institution," the supervisor informed her team at the morning briefing. "I'll speak to her myself." Relief spread like an invisible cloud as they went to their assigned floors.

The discussion also did not go well. After being told the woman volunteer must stop what she was telling the patients, the volunteer, with a flushed face and trembling hand, pulled off her smock and threw it on the floor.

Immediately, the flower volunteer almost flew like a threatening cloud toward the hospital entrance. Winter hadn't been kind this year, and several small patches of ice formed on the sharp edges of the hospital's granite steps. New shoes are traitors. One slip on the ice, and the volunteer's body weight worked to slant her backward as she fell. The edge of the granite was sufficient. There would be no more praying.

A MAYONNAISE JAR THERMOS

The wax paper was tautly pulled from the box and positioned along the serrated edge to cut as small a piece as possible. A faint zipping and then the box was placed on the linoleum-covered shelf in the kitchen. With the precision of an engineer, the small piece was placed over the open mayonnaise jar containing milk. The top was tightened to avoid tearing the paper. It would keep the pristine liquid safe from leaking should it shake too much on its intended journey. It was now going to third grade.

Third grade was when it all happened. Until that time, things were normal in my eyes. I never saw myself in my thick-soled, resoled, and resoled shoes as different. Years later, I would tell comical stories about those shoes that resembled the rungs on a rocking chair.

Now, in my tightly twisted braids, I was no different from the girl who wore banana curls in her hair. Of course, that was until the day we had to go to mass at 8 AM and receive holy communion.

To prepare for holy communion, we couldn't eat after midnight, so we had to bring our breakfast to school. The robust tan brick building had no cafeteria (we ate next to the boiler room), nor did it have a library or any science materials. But we had lots of depictions of bloody saints, eyes lying on plates, or large map-like colored sheets on stands that related acceptable, virginal Bible stories. Religion and etiquette took the place of math and science in our school.

In our ground-floor room, seated at our old wooden desks with the inkwell holes still prominent on each one and a shelf held in place by cast-iron filigree sides, I retrieved my breakfast from my paper bag. Mass was over and we'd all swallowed the dry host that stuck to the roof of our mouths. It was time for breakfast. My breakfast was different from other students' meals. I didn't know it.

The milk that my mother had given to me was in the mayonnaise jar filled one-third of the way up and accompanied by two slices of buttered white toast wrapped in wax paper. That was breakfast. I didn't give it a second thought and didn't look around to see what others had.

If I had looked around, I would have seen cartoon character lunch boxes that snapped open to reveal small thermoses, a piece of fruit, and a sandwich. Nothing was wrapped in wax paper.

But no one ever said anything. No one ever turned around and gave one of those disgusted looks or commented on what I was having for breakfast. Yes, it was laid out on the top of my desk, carefully placed atop the wax paper from the toast. We were all too polite. Those etiquette lessons we had four days a week drove that point home with a sledgehammer.

After breakfast, we had another chore, one that took place in every classroom throughout the school after each spring semester; repair, clean, and wrap.

Summer was coming and it was time to mend our books, removing stray pencil marks with an eraser, a bit of bleach on a matchstick for the ink spots, and clear tape for torn pages. Then, brown supermarket bags were cut and folded to serve as book covers. We wrapped our desks in newspaper tied with a string and we were off.

Of course, the boys had to clap erasers outside, lemon oil the teacher's desk, and wash down the blackboards. The room was pristine with a faint smell of that oil and ready for the fall.

Back to school in September, everything went fine until October when three women, in flowered dresses, wearing hats and white gloves, walked into the room. Their faces were plastered with artificial smiles as they looked out over our shining faces upturned to provide an appropriate audience. But a hint of their body language gave them away as they pulled back from where we sat. What were they here for? I don't think any of us knew.

I was sitting at the front of the class now because I was somewhat short, but I was also a favorite of our teacher, possibly because I was shy.

"Children, children, attention now to the ladies from the Mothers' Club. They have a special gift for one of you." Gift? What type of gift would they have?

One of the three took a single step closer to us, plunged her hand into an embroidered bag, and pulled out a small doll. Not much of a doll, but a doll just the same.

"And the lucky child is…(my name was called)." The three turned as though on lazy Susan turntables and faced me. I was the child recipient.

Of course, I did not know how to react as she pushed the doll onto my desk. I'd never had a doll and didn't want one, but I'd have to accept this one. Later, I would hear via the local grapevine that the poorest child in the class got a doll from the Mothers' Club each year. I was now designated as the poorest.

The grapevine provided another tidbit. The student with the highest average in class each spring semester got a prize. I'd only heard whispers, but I showed interest. Forget the doll. I wanted a prize.

It went that way until I graduated from elementary school. Each year I got the prize and that day of the doll built a fire of ambition that burns brightly still. I want prizes. Will I ever stop? Who knows?

WINTER'S QUICK FIX

Dangling streetlights are being tossed by the wind like lemon drops in the darkening evening sky. The occasional whistling sound isn't a train, but the unforgiving tempest whipping around the buildings on the town's nearly empty main street.

Snowflakes swirl around like confetti at a wedding. The street's few pedestrians lean into the wind as a lone dog scampers across the street, its tail between its legs, seeking shelter. Momentarily, it turns its head and gazes at Harry eye-to-eye. Is he danger or will he feed me?

What kind of life must that mutt have had? Harry pictures a place where the mutt wasn't cared for, was maybe even resented, and someone decided to dump him by the side of the road. How long had he been out in the cold?

Was he used to scrounging for scraps, being chased by restaurant kitchen workers raising sharp knives in his direction, and nearly sent flying by cars whizzing by him? Yeah, this dog hasn't had it easy, and who knows where it would end for him. If he's lucky, maybe some kind person will take pity on him and he'll find a new home. Maybe.

Turning his thoughts to his mission, Harry pulls himself up to his full height. Standing outside the jewelry store window aglow with its mirrors and bright lights, Harry has only one thing on his mind: getting warm and a few free meals—and he knows how to get what he needs. Empty pockets require creativity, and Harry has it.

He'll get what he wants. But now he reaches into his jacket pocket (which at the moment is not empty) for the meat loaf sandwich given to him by the woman in the soup kitchen.

"Here, let me put it in a bag for you so you can take it home," she said with a smile as she slipped the food in and smoothly folded the top.

Home? Home was a thousand miles and decades away. There would be no home for this sandwich.

Harry has felt what the stray must be feeling now. He understands a lack of belonging. The pangs of hunger, too, that come as you tense in the cold night.

Snow and small glittering ice drops cover the curly back of the animal that stands, unsure of the man in front of it.

Softly, Harry encourages him to stay and extends his hand, the sandwich clearly in view. Of course, this stray might be a bit more vicious than Harry thought, but he persists. The dog flinches. Lurching forward, it snatches the food, barely missing Harry's out-held fingers with his bared teeth. Running off, it squeezes through a fence hole and disappears.

Now, Harry returns to his desperate plan. This year, it's time to try. He pushes his hands deep into his jacket pockets to create a bulge that spells danger.

The woman is alone in the shop, scowling and scribbling in a ledger, and she wouldn't have noticed him if the bell on the door hadn't sounded. Harry thrusts the door open so hard it slams into one of the display cases. Her body posture changes into an immediate tense stance. It's almost as though she's received an order or command to stand up. No order has been given, but she knows what she must do in response to this hulking stranger.

She trembles, a display case her only support. Standing straight up so abruptly sends the ledger falling to the floor. Her hand remains curled around the pencil as though it were a knife, as she forces a smile and the usual greeting.

"Can I help you?" comes out of her suddenly dry mouth.

"Give me all those rings you've got here," Harry says in the most menacing tone he can muster. One hand with an outstretched finger points at the nearest case. As he speaks, he moves his fist in the bulging pocket. She wonders why she failed to follow her husband's orders to lock the door at closing time.

"And those watches, too, give me all of them! Put them in a bag." Harry's shouts almost scare him.

No one comes from the back room, and Harry knows they are alone and the woman will comply. A wave of cool relief slows his pounding heart. Everything is going as planned. But wait, she's taking a step to the side. Does she have something in mind? No. She's frightened.

Standing more than a foot taller than the woman, Harry gives the impression of solid muscles, and he steps forward in response to her action. Yes, he looks like someone a woman alone in a shop with expensive jewelry should fear. If she knew his true intent, Harry thinks to himself, she wouldn't be scared for a minute.

Her trembling hands begin to scoop up and slide the watches and the jewelry from the case into a bank night deposit bag she has near her on the counter. Her outstretched arm looks like the hoop with the golden ring on the merry-go-round Harry rode as a child.

He shoots his free hand out and snatches the swinging bag. A quick turn and he's out the door. The snowy bench in front of the shop is quickly dusted off and Harry sits down. OK, it's going to be just a short wait now while she calls the police.

The scenario plays as Harry knows it will. Here are the police. Harry delivers his prepared script ("The voices told me to do it."). The crying woman points to him, and then there's the quick trip in handcuffs to the hospital.

Harry knows who will be on duty to receive him; he's correct, as always. An intern, still green behind the ears, half-asleep and stumbling, comes toward him with a clipboard. Yes, he's prime for Harry's tale of paranoia. They always are at this time of night on weekends.

Assuming the posture that fits the mood of dejection he wants to display, Harry crouches over and whispers into the intern's ear.

"They tell me things," he says in a hushed voice, peering around as though in fear.

"What do they say to you?" The young man is ready to accept anything that will allow him to get back to bed after a twenty-four-hour shift.

"I can't say because they mumble, but it was that I had to take the jewelry in the store." Harry's voice dips lower as he pulls back a bit and watches the intern writing.

Yes, he knows the result: three hots and a cot for the winter. The poor dog should be so lucky, but at least he has that sandwich, Harry thinks to himself.

On the clipboard, the intern writes "paranoid schizophrenia" and signals for two burly men in white outfits to take Harry away. The darkened hallway swallows him up as the men hold his arms in their vice-like hands.

THE BIG BREAK

Alarm clocks make noise that penetrates thin walls, and if you want to stealthily filch your neighbor's copy of a weekly trade publication, an alarm clock is the last thing you want in your room.

The clever bit of swiftly snatching and as quickly perusing the columns of ads for actors had become a skill at which he was a perfectionist. You had to be, or you'd end up never making it in this business. Making it was all he had ever dreamed of since he was a little boy in elementary school.

The trade ad he was waiting for was here. Eyes widening, he tried to slow his heart, but it was no use. Blood was rushing through his body and sweat pulsed from his brow.

In bold type it read: "TV food commercial shoot, male/female actors, male 20s-30s, older woman, ethnic Italian family types."

It's all he wanted, and he fit the part. Finally, all these years of sitting and inputting data onto statistical charts for these guys. Now was his chance, and he was going to make a TV commercial, if it killed him.

He knows the part is right for him and he needs the money. His landlord's latest notice had a tone that was easily understood. But more than that, he needs the exposure this commercial provides for an actor. It is his chance to break through, to make it.

Enough sitting in those dark, smelly hallways waiting for a call into dimly lit old rehearsal rooms to be faced by a few guys just over their pimple-popping age who barely lift their heads and look at him like he's groceries. The remarks sound like they're looking at sides of beef, and they check him off on their clipboards as so many grocery items in a store.

A quick call, a request to come into work a bit late and he's got a shot at the role. The room over a betting parlor near a strip joint is barren except for that infamous table with three guys huddled behind it. Would he do for the part seemed to be the question they're mulling over with sideward glances as he stands in front of them, a man on a mission, but in his mind in front of a firing squad.

"Yeah, hair okay, skin not too dark. Straight teeth. Not too tall and kind of thin." In a sotto voce tone, one asks the other two, "But don't you think he's too old? He's got to be over thirty."

"Shhhh, he'll do for now," one barely whispers out of the side of his mouth.

"Thin, so people want momma to feed him, right?" Another snickers in a less-than-a-stage whisper. Loud enough to make him uncomfortable.

They don't offer him a chair. He's forced to stand before them as they roll their eyes up and down his body and his clothing.

"He doesn't smell, does he," one asks the other two. The three laugh with no regard for him.

"Okay, read this." A sheet of paper with three lines on it is pushed toward the edge of the table, almost fluttering to the floor. The reading is a bit bumpy, but he gets through it once.

"Yeah, that's all right and you look pretty much like what we need; you got that darkish complexion and that black hair. But we need more than you," the half-turned around youngest with the toothpick in his mouth utters almost into the air.

"We need more of you ethnic types. You know, your relative types and a momma, too. You got relatives? Yeah, we need relatives. Is that something you can do, kid?"

The "kid" comment smacked his ears like a sock with a roll of coins in it. Relatives? Did he have relatives? What was this, anyway?

"And not just any relatives. You know, we need cousins and uncles, and they need to be dressed as though they're hanging around the house waiting for momma to make dinner. Nothing fancy, you know, just plain clothes. The momma type has to be special, too. Got it, kid? Not just any momma type, one you'd see hanging out a window yelling for the kids to come in for supper. Got it, kid? She has to be like an old Sophia

Loren type with that sexiness, but older. Get the picture, kid?" And the description went on for another ten minutes.

If the momma type were described in greater detail, he'd need a pad to write it all down. The guy wanted something he didn't have, but he'd learned years ago from an acting coach that you always tell them you have what they want, even if you don't.

The older momma-type had to meet the requirements as the toothpick-chewing, just-out-of- college guy, or was it just out of high school, was outlining in detail as though he were talking to a moron.

She had to have gray hair, "but not too gray," be slightly overweight "but charming and with a good, hearty but sexy laugh." And then he added, "You know, like the momma you want to take back to the apartment, get it?" The wink cinched it. It sounded like he was describing a dish on a plate in a restaurant. He was food and these guys were the meat grinders.

Back at the office, Tony rounded up the leftover evening staff around the coffee wagon and selected types he could use for his ruse. To each, he cautiously whispered an invitation. They loved it! Commercials? All of them were eager and trouped over to the rehearsal hall with him a few evenings later. No hitches and they loved his "momma" who acted like an older sexy Loren. Even the pimply one was impressed.

"Okay there are no lines, so all you have to do is stand around the way we place you and momma has to yell for you to come in. Just a yell, that's all. Okay, momma, let me hear you yell."

Inhaling deeply and almost popping a button on her voluptuous bosom in the process, "Momma" let out a scream that made them all jump. Who knew she could yell like that?

"Yeah," she chirped, "I used to call the rest of the family to dinner because my momma was too busy, so I had lots of practice. Haven't used that in years."

Cattle call over, they disappeared into the night until the next evening when Tony would see them at work again.

In the office, in an area off to the side where he wouldn't be heard, he stared at the lump of black plastic before him. Devoid of any humanity, its electronic circuits and plain numbered buttons told tales unwanted. The memories and turn-downs felt flung in his face by the unit.

Forcing himself to push his hand forward, he picked up the receiver, punched in the numbers slowly and waited. It was the waiting that never seemed to end. Now it was even longer.

Today, the office evening staff was chatting about something that brought brief waves of laughter to fill the empty space. What could it be?

He listened but all he heard was, "Yeah, today, this morning." And then the other sentences came tumbling out and he got that knot in his stomach.

"Yes, she called in today and told her boss that he could take the job and shove it. Can you believe she'd use language like that? After how she's always presented herself as though she's European royalty and we're simply American riffraff. Yeah, that slight accent did help. Was it real, do you think?"

Laughter louder now with nodding of heads and hands held to mouths to suppress laughs too much for an office.

A cheery voice responded to his call. "Oh, yeah, Tony. The reading was perfect, and everyone worked together marvelously, especially that woman you brought and we called momma," the agent told him in a voice eager to get off the phone. "They made the choice and the woman you found to play your mother was signed for the commercial."

He held himself back and murmured, "You mean," he replied haltingly, "I didn't get a role, but she did?"

The "momma" woman, a lowly clerk, had never acted in her life, had money from her husband's estate, and hadn't wanted to go to the audition. He had to plead with her to accompany him. They wanted ethnic types and one was needed for the momma.

He promised to input data for her, to take her out to dinner, to do anything she wanted, if she'd only come with him. For God's sake, he'd even sleep with her if she'd agree to do this one favor. Well, maybe that wouldn't have been a favor only for her. She was a little Loren-ish.

The commercial ran for three months and the checks rolled into her bank account. Now she had an agent and was a regular on ads when they wanted a sexy, ethnic momma type. She fit into this new life perfectly. Her only competition had died months ago, and she was the sole choice for the roles.

Enough with the rejections, he thought, with being told he was too short, too thin, his hair wasn't right, he was getting older, and he had a Queens' accent. Enough!

Twelve floors up, the expansive glass window looked back at him, blank as always, but now with a special message. He understood.

A GOOD THING

Timing traffic lights along the major avenues is a quick way to navigate without stopping, but the speed must be timed to exactly match when the light will change from green to yellow, followed by red. Drivers on the side streets are timing the lights as well and hitting the gas as red turns to green. They have all learned or are taught the art of rolling at that carefully calibrated speed that matches the color changes. But tonight, two women's timing will be off.

The streets are free of pedestrians as the cars are almost sliding down the wide avenues like grease running down a hill. Everything is going so smoothly.

Keen eyes watch the traffic lights turn in a synchronized, anticipated row of green to yellow to red. But one driver, off the boulevard, is impatient, pressing the accelerator to jump the light.

From the side street, Angela is starting forward too soon onto the boulevard before her green light appears. The result is an unfortunate collision of brands in the middle of the intersection.

Shouting begins, finger-pointing, and a quick call for a police car and an ambulance is made, although no injuries are apparent to any of the parties in the cars. It all begins and ends quickly, and everyone goes their separate ways.

The too-eager driver, Angela, looks over at her friend who was too drunk to drive her mother's car. Now the car limps home with serious damage.

The mother isn't told her daughter was too drunk to drive, and the woman is not pleased once the car is at her house. But she says little to Angela or her daughter, who both stagger into the house. Angela will be spending the night.

A few weeks later, calls are made regarding insurance reimbursement and a lawsuit for injuries allegedly suffered. Angela and the car's owner, the drunken friend's mother, are expected to appear at the courthouse to hear the charges and make their pleas. They wait in the hallway, not knowing what is happening inside the chamber, for some sign showing what is to come next.

The friend's mother is reassuring Angela. "Don't worry, kid, it'll all be fine. I know this is upsetting, but believe me, it's gonna be fine." The woman's gravelly voice has a degree of unexpected confidence. Everything would be fine. But how does she know that so emphatically?

The large wooden door to the courtroom opens suddenly and a man in a green Brioni knit golf shirt comes walking out as though he owns the building. His head cocked, he whispers, "It's fine, it's over," to the woman.

"So, wha happened, Butchie?" The woman looks at him in a way that bespeaks an understanding the daughter's friend doesn't have. "It was a good thing. They dropped the case, Anna. The other driver's dead, so there's no witness for the plaintiff and there's no evidence against your car."

His tone is matter-of-fact as he shrugs his shoulders, lifting an upraised palm that highlights the yellow diamond pinky ring. After all, Anna is the daughter of the most important guy at the local social club, and Butchie wants to help her out.

Now Anna turns her attention to the young woman beside her. There's no reason for her daughter's friend to be upset and she wants to help her feel better. It's always been her way to soothe things over and she's doing it again.

Throughout her life she's been in these situations before, such as when her boyfriend, Leftie, was shot in a bar fight. Anna was his wife's friend who came to comfort her in the hospital. Thinking to herself, she knows how to give her daughter's friend absolution for this accident. It will be an invitation to her card party. The specialness of the invitation alone is clear evidence of forgiveness.

"See, I told you honey, it would all be fine. Tonight, we're gonna play cards at my house. You're coming, right?" This was no question. No one ever turned down this invitation.

The house was in a neighborhood of homes of Anna's relatives, all bought by a generous grandmother. Each child was given a home when the child married, and the grandmother handled the family money. All the players at the game are either related or members of the local social club.

This crew of childhood friends has a regular Wednesday evening poker game. It's on Wednesday because Thursday is for taking girlfriends to clubs to show them off. The invitation is incredible and Angela knows it. No one gets an invitation to these card games. They are closely held events where few sit in. Offers are extended and never refused.

"Come on Angela, you want to join the game?" As she says it, Anna puts her arm around the young woman in a show of affection. It is left as an open question, requiring no response.

At the card game that night, the question is the same, but this time in front of the intensely interested men seated around the large dining room table. Anna is the lone woman at the table.

"No, I don't know how to play cards. I've tried and I just can't do it."

An unbelievable remark. The group laughs and gives her permission with upraised hands and waves to leave the room without joining. But first a pastry and coffee from the sideboard. After all, she is a guest, even if she was driving Anna's car when it was demolished.

"OK then, you go watch TV with the girls while I lose all my money." The throaty smoker's voice blends in with others' equally roughened by years of cigarettes and Cuban cigars.

Anna's "girl" visitors, wives of the players, arrange themselves on the furniture and make fun of the shows or adjust their makeup. No one dares interrupt the game. The intensity in the room is palpable as the smoke and the language turns the air blue.

Then the car incident comes into focus.

The cigarette smoke swirls as one player yells out. "Hey, Butchie, where'd you get that outfit? Did it fall off a truck?"

"Yeah, off a truck," comes the response with a smirk. "You got a few suits, didn't you off one of those dumb trucks?" The wisecrack is well-received with more joking.

Now the laughter rises and falls like a verbal tide in the room. But the short-lived joke is followed by another question.

As the laughing dies down, the man dares to ask. "So, what happened with that car accident Anna's daughter's friend had? There was a court date today, right? You went with Anna, cause she owns the car, right?"

Butchie works his Cuban around his mouth as he feigns little interest, lasering his cards. The slightly lifted brow tells another story.

"No, I met Anna there. Yeah, the other driver's dead, so the case was dropped." The reply comes from behind Butchie's fanned-out cards.

"It was a real tragedy," he says with no note of emotion. Again, the chewed cigar is shifted in position in his moist mouth as though he were about to do a magic trick with it.

"Yeah, a real tragedy. I loved that car," Anna says almost in a moan. The sense of loss for her is a psychic blow no one would understand. She loved that car. Her father gave it to her as a Christmas present before he got that diagnosis.

Anna never lifts her head as she responds and continues to throw chips into the pot piling up in the center of the table. Yes, she's losing all her money tonight, as usual.

The inquisitor continues. "No, yeah, a tragedy about the car, but the driver ... Who knew? But, Anna, she hit your car. Right? It was her fault you lost that car, and you loved that car. Right? You loved that car?"

All the players know the accident is a closed matter. They nod in almost bobblehead comedic agreement that she loved that car. A mixture of soft, affirming comments stops the game, but only briefly.

The men know how much Anna loved that car. It was like one of her children and she'll take a long time getting over the loss.

Toward the side of the room, a newspaper is draped over a chair. The front page tells a story no one in the group needs or wants to read.

A disturbing photo of a young woman's body lying in an apartment doorway takes up much of the front page.

The bold headline screams about the homicide as though it were announcing the bombing of Pearl Harbor.

According to the newspaper account, the young woman, recuperating from a recent car accident, had answered the doorbell at her ground-floor apartment the night before. Opening the door, she was confronted by a man.

A handgun was pointed directly at her left eye, the trigger pulled, and she fell backward. The shooter turned slowly and got into a waiting car.

The media would surmise it was a disgruntled boyfriend, but they would be wrong. One passerby's comments were noted in the article. The witness told police in a quivering voice that he thought the man was wearing some sort of flashy, designer golf shirt. But the trembling man wasn't sure because it was dark. "I can't be sure," he reiterated repeatedly.

Oh, how Anna loved that car.

MISTRESS

The shiny ball struggled to make its way across the Persian rug in the entryway. A slightly stooped gray-haired woman tiptoed after it, and, with a slight groan, bent over to pick it up.

"Here, I've got it, Jason."

The high-pitched shouting slipping under the library door is alerting the nanny that something is coming. Clips of the argument carry words of warning.

Mistress has a special look, and she used it well. Anyone looking at her would have stopped in their tracks before paying attention to what she said. Her lipstick was a deep red, her black dress cinched tight around her waist. The material of her dress was smooth and soft, like a thousand silk spiders, their legs skittering over one another and weaving a web of silk to repel the outside world. Her perfume was intoxicating.

"No, we're not paying for it! I want her gone and I want it now! I won't have her walking around with her hair falling out, frightening the children. She's got to be gone this week. Isn't this the week she begins the treatments? You've got to tell her today before you go on any trips."

Any responses uttered were indistinguishable. But the storm was coming before the clouds had ever shown in the entryway and the nanny knew it.

Called into the library, a low-toned dismissal quickly dispatched the man's guilt as he scribbled a check and dropped it on the desk. The deed was done, and his shame was well-hidden. She had a diagnosis of cancer and she had to go. No medical payments would be made. His wife wouldn't have it.

Standing by the front door now, Mistress swiveled on one heel and lowered her sunglasses to look at the older woman.

"Marie, the children are going to my sister's for a few weeks. We won't be needing you. You can go on your vacation. I see that you've already got your bags packed by the back entrance and our check."

Framed in the doorway, she is smiling, a goddess in her prime, a woman in her thirties, her hair is blindingly radiant blonde, the kind of woman that men cannot remove their eyes from and you don't approach. Mistress continued as though in an afterthought, "Oh, and before you leave, Marie, would you see if cook would save one of those wonderful little cakes, you know the new recipe she got? I'd love to have one after golf today."

The red soles of her shoes peeked for a moment as they met the crushed pebble driveway where the door to the Maybach is opened for her.

Cook will be busily making jam from a recipe. She is determined to prepare a sticky, sweet mixture like strawberry jam. Small cakes, waiting on a tray, are to be stuffed with this special jam as bait for rats by the pool house. The gardener already spotted them slipping onto the grounds.

A basket full of mangrove "apples," the main ingredient, waits on the prep sink. Carefully, the gardener's rubber-gloved hands select them for the cook in her gloved hands to peel.

"Careful, Hank, you don't want any of this stuff on your skin. It will work its way right through and, if you're lucky, you'll only be sick as a dog and not dead like those rats will be shortly."

A laugh echoes in the large ceramic and stainless room, bouncing off the walls as the cook forgets the danger and she attempts to cover her mouth. Even gloved hands could be dangerous. A darting move by the gardener pushes her hand away and she is safe to continue cooking.

Shortly a bubbling brew is coaxed into a glass jar and jam sits on the kitchen table, left to cool. The cook is distracted elsewhere and leaves the jam to take to the tool shed later.

Mistress already said she wants a snack when she returns but her husband, back home before her, spots the jam. The scent of freshly baked bread and warm jam is too much to resist and he mounds the jam on a thick slice of sourdough bread.

The taste tingles his tongue with its delightful sweetness until it inflames his throat, choking his breath and he runs for water from the sink near the upper kitchen door. The slick loafers' soles slip on a bit of apple fruit peel sending him plummeting over the kitchen's short second-floor railing and onto the stone patio below. Not a sound disturbs the quiet cool of the garden as the rats slither from the pool house.

But death is never so complete. Everything Mistress did, the husband stalking, the romancing, the tricking into a marriage with a false pregnancy, has been for naught. After the funeral, Mistress now discovers her husband had a second family and left everything in his will to them, rather than her. She gets a small beach house in a neighboring community with a suitably small monthly allowance. A new husband search will begin.

THE DAY THE BULLS CAME

Red splashes and shimmering threads spread slowly, randomly, in a lazy fashion across the Victorian white bathroom tile floor like tiny veins. The dark-red stream continued to widen, pushing forward in short pulses, overflowing each octagonal tile even as the propelling force grows weaker. Soon the floor and the walls would be a disturbing mass of small colored rivers reaching out from large pools, dripping finger-like splotches on the fixtures. It would be over within minutes; the deed would be done but never truly over.

The memory of it all would remain locked away in a closet in my mind.

I'd be questioned at the district attorney's office about an offensive comment aimed at me after I saw a toddler slapped in a highchair. I still didn't know why I was being questioned. All I remembered was sitting in blissful ignorance, watching a bowl of grated potatoes turn from tan to brown to black as my home seemed to explode with men in suits.

I wouldn't be going to school this day, or for a week afterward, and for our services, each of us would be given seven dollars.

Every day we arrived by overheated subway. We were led by armed guards to the room where we would be virtual prisoners, waiting for our turn to be called as witnesses, to be questioned by three defense attorneys. The defendant, our former neighbor and now an alleged baby killer, would be brought in wearing an ill-fitting blue suit, his wrists handcuffed behind him.

Yes, they'd given him three public defenders. Quite unusual under any circumstances, and I don't, to this day, know why he required that many. Could they have been working pro bono, or were they drawn in by the opportunity for a career-making high-profile case?

The newspapers were devouring every detail they could eke out of anyone near us or the case. We were forbidden to talk to anyone. My older sister threw a sweater over my head to cover me as we left each day, the photographers scrambling for their shots. I was being protected as she had always protected anyone in our family. Flashbulbs exploded as though we were at a Hollywood premiere, and the densely packed crowd tried to hold us back for more photographs.

Headlines and large photos were the lifeblood of the newspapers. Murderer or "baby killer" were two favorite headlines. With a young girl as a witness, papers were selling out. All three of the local papers featured the trial and the killer. But we knew none of this because they mandated us not to look at television or read any newspapers or speak to anyone about the trial.

There was no escape for us from the witness room. We were locked in. If you needed to use the restroom, you were accompanied by a guard who then stood outside the door. I won't deny that, for me, this was more than disquieting. I had a friend whose uncle snuck into her house and stood outside the bathroom door whenever she went in to urinate. It scared her, and I carried that fear, too.

Our one break was at noon. Two armed guards would come to escort us to the coffee shop across the street from the courthouse.

"Okay, it's time to eat. Let's go," one ordered as he opened the door.

The short walk wasn't without incident, what with the reporters and photographers pushing them for access and the guards holding them back with their batons. A crowd was always waiting for us when we emerged from the front door and then down the polished steps to the walkway and across the street.

The air in the coffee shop was thick with blue cigarette smoke and the smell of stale tobacco and frying grease. The reporters and staff ate, smoked, and gulped down iced tea or coffee. Ashtrays were filled to the brim even before we entered, and the tables themselves carried the burns of cigarettes and cigars carelessly placed there. This wasn't a place you'd choose for lunch by any means, but it was convenient and cheap, and the city ran a tab for trial witnesses.

"Order a hot meal, dear," our landlady coaxed me as she leaned over in a conspiratorial posture and whispered close to my ear. *"They're paying for it, so you might as well have a good meal."*

I was sick to my stomach from the anxiety and experience of the trial. How could I eat anything? Just the thought of food was making me sick, and I had lost weight already from my lack of appetite.

When the food arrived, it was a slab of Salisbury steak swimming in a thick dark-brown goop, an ice cream scoop of mashed potatoes, and a large helping of bright-green peas and orange carrots. The color of both the peas and the carrots stood out in sharp contrast to the rest of the unappealing mess.

I toyed with the food, pushing it around with my fork, eating just a bit of the mashed potatoes, and hoped that the guard would signal that it was time to return to our wood-paneled dungeon. As for the rest of my luncheon companions, I was totally oblivious—they might as well not have existed at all. Out of the corner of my eye, I saw the guard move uncomfortably, shifting his weight a bit, and I knew we would be free at last.

"Okay," he said in a stern tone as he hovered over the table, *"time to go back. Finish up and let's go."*

Why were we here and how had it all begun—the murder? It would be almost three decades before I could pry any of the grisly story out of my mother. Yes, I'd gotten her to drink two orange blossoms drinks and she was a woman who never drank, but this drink was the means to open the story up to me. And it was a horrific story that I carry to this day as though it had just happened.

The meals, the witness room, and the disturbing tale my mother would tell about that blood-stained bathroom are all written in my memory banks like some grim detective story. Oh, by the way, in our neighborhood, the police detectives were called the "bulls"—when they came, someone was going to be beaten. The bulls were feared. There would be no beatings, but perhaps there had been, as I would see momentarily after the complete takeover of our home. They swarmed in, grabbed the phone, and began documenting the scene of the killing. Before they left with their suspect, I would notice the wide red line running from his swollen nose to his chin.

It took a while for my mother to tell the story. It was hard to believe, even though I had lived it. Attempting to provide a cover story, the child's mother called my mother for assistance. A little three-year-old boy had been murdered by his father in the next-door apartment—this was the reality. The bathroom and child's room were bathed in blood, but the child's mother insisted it was an "accident." She said the boy had fallen out of his crib, a terrible lie.

The boy's father wasn't in the room when my mother arrived to view a scene that brought tears to her eyes. Horribly bent out of shape like a broken rag doll, the child lay on the floor with no blanket or pajamas, only a stained diaper. My mother found that curious. Where was the father?

Our house had a connecting basement to their cellar; this was where the father intended to burn the evidence. He couldn't pry the door open to access the furnace, thus thwarting his plan. Instead, he tried to stuff the bloody blanket and clothing into an open space beneath the overhead boards—that didn't work, either.

The details of the room and the child were something from which I had been spared, but my mother would now begin to provide some of them. The story would be told to me this day as we sat in a quiet seashore restaurant with large open windows and a fresh breeze filling the room. A shore dinner sat before my mother, and she picked at it as she related the details—many of which I've managed to hide from myself.

How did it end? He was found guilty of manslaughter and sentenced to prison. His girlfriend, the boy's mother, said she would wait for him. Wait for the man who murdered your son? My mother couldn't believe it, but that was the woman's decision.

Afterward, I would return to elementary school and everything would go on as before.

Books by Dr. Patricia A. Farrell

How to Be Your Own Therapist

It's Not All in Your Head: Anxiety, Depression, Mood Swings and Multiple Sclerosis

A Social Security Disability Psychological Claims Handbook: A simple guide to understanding your SSD claim for psychological impairments and unraveling the maze of decision making

A Social Security Disability Psychological Claims Guidebook for Children's Benefits

The Disability Accessible US Parks in All 50 States: A Comprehensive Guide

Birding in the US NOW!: A birding guide for individuals with disabilities

About Author

P. A.Farrell (Dr. Farrell's fiction-writing pseudonym) is a published author of multiple self-help books and videos, a licensed psychologist, a former WebMD psychologist expert/consultant, a former medical consultant for Social Security Disability Determinations, a psychiatric researcher at Mt. Sinai Medical Center (NYC), and an educator who has taught on the college, graduate and post-graduate levels, appeared on national TV shows, and on international, regional and national syndicated radio shows and in print media in national newspapers and magazines. She is also a top health writer for Medium.com publications. Her fiction writing (flash fiction) has been and continues to be published online and in print.

Dr. Farrell has a website (http://www.drfarrell.net), is a consultant to pharmaceutical firms, writes continuing education modules for mental healthcare professionals, has contributed to USMLE medical school prep courses, writes daily tweets (@drpatfarrell), has a YouTube channel with helpful videos on multiple topics and is a biographee in *Who's Who in the World, Who's Who in America* and *Who's Who in American Women*.

A member of The American Psychological Association and the SAG-AFTRA union, Dr. Farrell is a former board member of the NJ Board of Psychological Examiners, a former psychiatry preceptor at UMDNJ, and a former board of directors' member of Bergen Pines Hospital.

Don't miss out!

Visit the website below and you can sign up to receive emails whenever P. A. Farrell publishes a new book. There's no charge and no obligation.

https://books2read.com/r/B-A-JNWAB-ONBPC

BOOKS 2 READ

Connecting independent readers to independent writers.

Also by P. A. Farrell

Unexpected Short Tales of Surprise

Watch for more at www.drfarrell.net.

About the Author

P. A. Farrell is a psychologist and published author with McGraw-Hill, Springer Publishing, Cafe Lit, Ravens Perch, Humans of the World, Active Muse, Free Spirit Publishing, Scarlet Leaf Review, 100 Word Project, Woodcrest Magazine, Confetti, and LitBreak. She's a top health writer for Medium.com, has published self-help books, and is a board member of Clinics4Life. She lives on the East Coast of the US.

Read more at www.drfarrell.net.

www.ingramcontent.com/pod-product-compliance
Lightning Source LLC
Chambersburg PA
CBHW031124160726
47989CB00016B/1374